The Sorcerer's Apprentice

Story by Neil Morris
Taken from the Walt Disney Company's
film, *Fantasia*

Hippo Books
Scholastic Children's Books
London

Scholastic Children's Books,
Scholastic Publications Ltd,
7-9 Pratt Street, London, NW1 0AE, UK

Scholastic Inc.,
730 Broadway, New York, NY 10003, USA

Scholastic Canada Ltd,
123 Newkirk Road, Richmond Hill,
Ontario, Canada L4C 3G5

Ashton Scholastic Pty Ltd,
P O Box 579, Gosford, New South Wales,
Australia

Ashton Scholastic Ltd,
Private Bag 1, Penrose, Auckland,
New Zealand

First published by Scholastic Publications Ltd, 1992
by arrangement with the Walt Disney Company

Copyright © Disney

ISBN 0 590 55055 1

Typeset by Flying Colours (London) Limited

Printed in Spain by Mateu Cromo,
Madrid

There was once a great sorcerer who knew all there was to know about magic. The sorcerer had a tall magic hat. When he wore the hat, he was able to cast spells of all kinds.

He could imagine a bat and make one appear. Then he could change the bat into a beautiful butterfly, just by thinking about it. Only the sorcerer knew how to do this, and only he could make things appear and disappear. With one swish of his hands, the butterfly would vanish.

The sorcerer had an apprentice named Mickey, who was working hard to learn all about magic. He did all the work in the sorcerer's castle.

He swept the floors,

chopped the wood

and carried water from the well.

Mickey often thought
how good it would be if
he didn't have to work
so hard.

One day, when the sorcerer went off for a nap, he left his hat on the table. Mickey saw the hat and realized at once that this was his great opportunity. He ran to the stairs to check that the sorcerer had definitely gone, and then tiptoed back to the table. Mickey snatched up the hat and put it on his head.

Looking around, Mickey saw an old broom leaning against the wall. He decided to cast a spell on the broom. So, copying his master, he thought very hard and pointed his fingers at the broom.

Slowly the broom began to move! First it grew feet. Then, as Mickey went on casting his spell, it grew arms and hands.

Mickey pointed to two empty buckets and the broom
picked them up. When Mickey walked over to the steps,
the broom marched after him. Soon they reached the well

where the broom filled the buckets with water and followed
Mickey back down the steps. When the broom had poured
the water into a big tub, it marched back up the steps with
the empty buckets.

As the broom worked, Mickey danced around the room. The sorcerer's apprentice will never have to work again, he thought to himself.

While the broom went on filling buckets and pouring water, Mickey sat down on the sorcerer's big chair. He put his feet up on the table and yawned. Soon he was fast asleep.

Mickey dreamed that he was the greatest sorcerer in the world. When he pointed at stars in the sky, they twinkled more brightly than ever. He found he could guide the stars like a conductor leading an orchestra. He sent comets circling the heavens. Sizzling fragments fell into the ocean.

In his dream, Mickey stood on a rock and conducted with his hands. He made lightning flash and huge waves crash. The sea surged up from below.

15

Suddenly something cold and wet woke Mickey up. It was a splash of water. Another splash knocked Mickey out of the chair. There was water everywhere! The broom was still pouring bucketfuls into the tub. But the tub was full — it was overflowing and flooding the castle.

Mickey splashed through the water to the steps and tried
to stop the broom. But the broom just pushed right past
him. Mickey grabbed one of the buckets, but the broom
wouldn't let go.

18

It emptied Mickey into the tub and then threw another bucket of water in his face! Poor Mickey wished he knew how to make the magic end. Surely there must be a way to stop the broom?

Just then, Mickey saw an axe by the door. He grabbed it and ran after the broom. Quickly he chopped the broom to pieces. Mickey thought it was all over. But he was in for a terrible surprise.

The chopped bits of wood started to move. Soon each one
turned into a new broom, carrying buckets of water.
Mickey couldn't believe it.

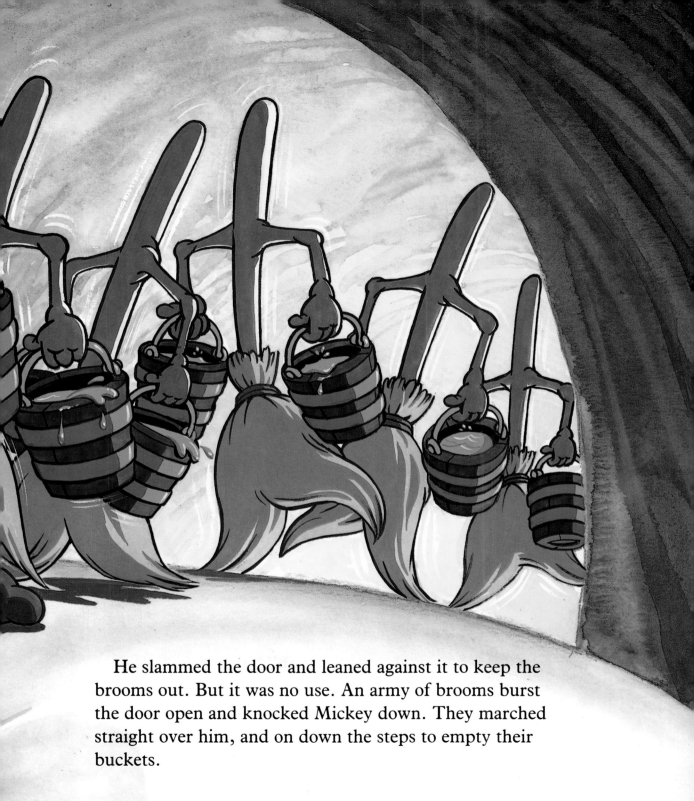

He slammed the door and leaned against it to keep the brooms out. But it was no use. An army of brooms burst the door open and knocked Mickey down. They marched straight over him, and on down the steps to empty their buckets.

There were brooms and more brooms, buckets and more buckets. In a great line, they poured and poured. Mickey picked up an empty bucket and started bailing water out of the window. But the water was getting deeper and deeper. Mickey could only just keep his head above it.

As the brooms marched on, carrying more and more buckets, Mickey soon found himself *under* water. He swam to the surface and grabbed the sorcerer's Book of Magic as it floated by. Frantically he flipped the pages of the book, searching for a way to stop the brooms. But the water was

whirling round so fast that Mickey couldn't read the words.
He clung to the book as it went round and round in the
water. Spinning faster and faster, Mickey was caught in a
giant whirlpool. Now there was nothing he could do.

At that moment a large shadow appeared on the wall. It was the sorcerer! He looked furious as he raised his arms in a commanding gesture. The water drained away from the steps. The sorcerer raised his arms again and again until at last the water and the brooms disappeared completely.

Only one broom was left, and that was the old broom leaning against the wall. The sorcerer frowned as he looked down at his apprentice. Mickey quickly took off the sorcerer's magic hat and very carefully straightened it out. The sorcerer grabbed the hat.

Mickey knew he had been foolish. After all, how could a mere apprentice expect suddenly to become a sorcerer? He looked up at the sorcerer and smiled sheepishly. But the sorcerer did not smile back. He was still very angry.

Mickey knew the best thing he could do was to go back to work at once. So he picked up the two buckets and tiptoed towards the steps. As Mickey passed by, the sorcerer raised the broom and gave him a smack to help him on his way. Mickey flew through the air, landed on his feet and ran off to get on with his work.